Words to Know Before Yo...

aquarium

coiled

nervously

nowhere

proudly

reptile

slither

suddenly

wrapped

www.rourkepublishing.com

Edited by Luana K. Mitten
Illustrated by Sarah Conner
Art Direction and Page Layout by Renee Brady

Library of Congress Cataloging-in-Publication Data

Picard Robbins, Maureen
 Snakes in Third Grade / Maureen Picard Robbins.
    p. cm. -- (Little Birdie Books)
 ISBN 978-1-61741-828-0 (hard cover) (alk. paper)
 ISBN 978-1-61236-032-4 (soft cover)
 Library of Congress Control Number: 2011924710

Rourke Publishing
Printed in China, Voion Industry
   Guangdong Province
042011
042011LP

www.rourkepublishing.com - rourke@rourkepublishing.com
Post Office Box 643328 Vero Beach, Florida 32964

Snakes In Third Grade!

snakes

By Maureen Picard Robbins

Illustrated by Sarah Conner

Mrs. Brewster placed Red, the new class snake, in Lizzie's hands

On the chalkboard:

$1 \times 7 = 7$

$2 \times 7 = 14$

$3 \times 7 = 21$

$4 \times 7 = 28$

$5 \times 7 = 35$

$6 \times 7 = 4$

$7 \times 7 = 4$

$8 \times 7 = 5$

$9 \times 7 =$

$10 \times 7 =$

"Is it slimy?" Jack asked.

"No! It's cool and dry." Lizzie said. "Do you want to feel it?"

"It's okay," said Jack nervously.

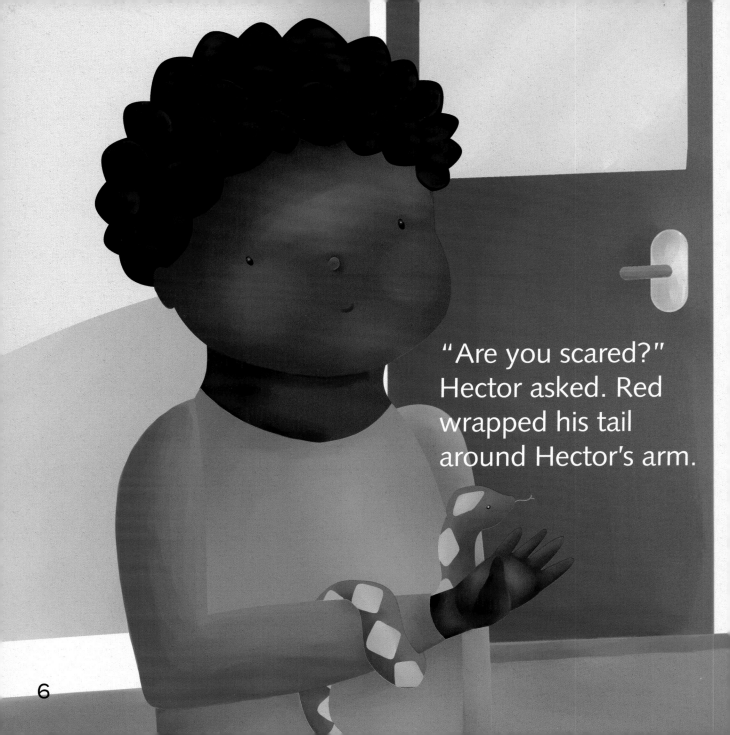

"Are you scared?" Hector asked. Red wrapped his tail around Hector's arm.

6

"No, of course not! I'm no scaredy-cat," said Jack. But he didn't touch the snake.

7

The next morning Jack arrived at school early. Instead of going to the library or to the playground, he sneaked into his dark classroom. The light behind Red's aquarium shined.

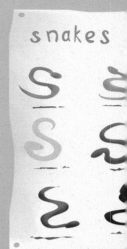

snakes

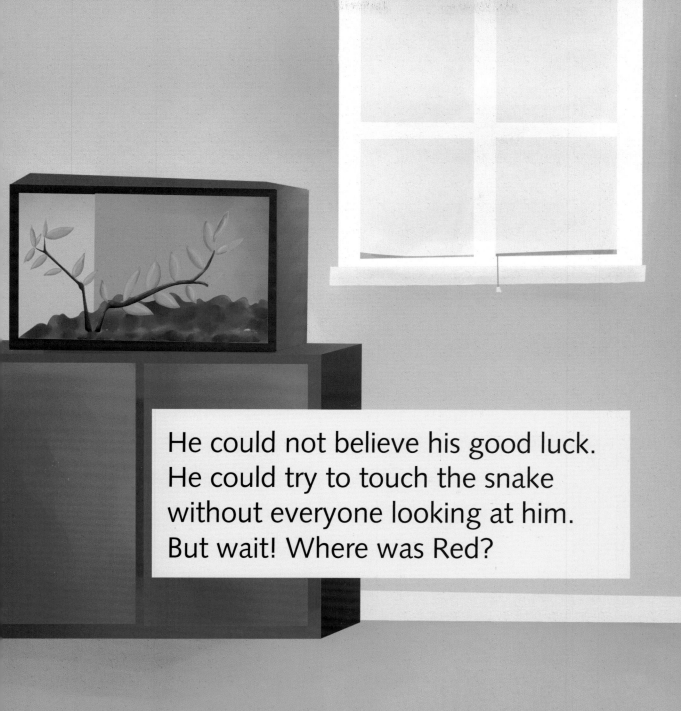

He could not believe his good luck.
He could try to touch the snake
without everyone looking at him.
But wait! Where was Red?

to be found. Red had escaped!

The two looked into the glass
cage and Mrs. Brewster saw the
problem. There was no snake.
"Oh dear," said Mrs. Brewster.

14

At that moment the rest of the
class filed into the classroom.
"Watch out!" cried Mrs. Brewster.
"Red's escaped!"

15

Hector searched the library book baskets. Lizzie peered under the heaters. She asked, "Jack, why are you just standing there?"

Jack said, with his tongue sticking out, "I'm trying do to what snakes do and taste the air."

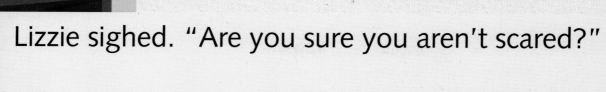

Lizzie sighed. "Are you sure you aren't scared?"

"I'm not, I told you!" Jack gulped and helped his friends search for Red.

The class searched for Red until lunchtime when Mrs. Brewster said, "We need to eat lunch. I'm sure Red will turn up soon."

18

Jack, Hector, and Lizzie sat at their desks and opened their lunch boxes.

"Yikes!" Jack gasped. There was Red, coiled around his water bottle!

Red slithered off the water bottle and around Jack's arm.

"You're right, you're not scared!" Lizzie was surprised.

Jack grinned proudly. No one was more surprised than him.

After Reading Activities

You and the Story...

Have you ever held a snake?

If you have, what did it feel like? If you have not, what do you think it would feel like?

What kind of pet would you like to have in your classroom?

Words You Know Now...

Several of the words below have endings such as –ed and – ly. On a piece of paper write each of the words with an added ending and then rewrite each of the words without its added ending. Does this change the meaning of the word?

aquarium	reptile
coiled	slither
nervously	suddenly
nowhere	wrapped
proudly	

You Could... Write About Your Favorite Class Pet

- What type of pet would you like in your classroom?

- What would you like to name the class pet?

- Make a list of everything your class will need to take care of it.

- If you already have a class pet, write about your class pet.

About the Author

Maureen Picard Robins writes poetry and books for kids and adults. She is an assistant principal at a New York City middle school. She lives in one of the five boroughs of New York City with her husband and daughters.

About the Illustrator

Sarah Conner is an illustrator living in London with her cat Berni. When she's not at her drawing-board (or computer!), she enjoys taking walks in London's beautiful parks, having picnics, knitting and gardening.